WWRT

What Went Right Today?℠

Written by
Joan Buzick & Lindy Judd

Illustrated by
James Kevin Sullivan

Music by
Joan Buzick

Making important information memorable®

A Buz-Land Presentations Book

Published by Buz-Land Presentations, Inc.
Scotch Plains, New Jersey USA 07076

Library of Congress Control Number: 2005903821

Publisher's Cataloging-In-Publication Data
(Prepared by The Donohue Group, Inc.)

Buzick, Joan.
    WWRT [kit] : what went right today? / written by Joan Buzick & Lindy Judd ; illustrated by James Kevin Sullivan ; music by Joan Buzick.

    1 book, 1 sound disc ; cm.
    Portion of title : What went right today
    ISBN-13: 978-0-9766990-0-2
    ISBN-10: 0-9766990-0-1

    1. Children's songs. 2. Life skills--Songs and music. 3. Conduct of life--Songs and music. 4. Parent and child--Songs and music. 5. Songs. 6. Life skills. 7. Conduct of life. 8. Parent and child. I. Judd, Lindy. II. Sullivan, James Kevin, 1964- III. Title. IV. Title: What went right today

M1992 .B89 2005
781.58   2005903821

Printed in Korea
10 9 8 7 6 5 4 3 2 1

To George and Elsie Buzick
&
Malcolm and Ethel Mae Judd

Who gave us our love of music, learning, humor,
and who always knew what went right today.

−JB & LJ

For Sully

Who taught me about printing, drawing, playing cards and taking the path less traveled.

". . . stand me now and ever in good stead."

−JKS

ACKNOWLEDGMENTS

There are many people who have contributed their ideas and time to make this book a success. We want to recognize them all, fully knowing we will miss someone.

First, are the administrators, teachers, parents and especially the students of Little Fiddler Academy, Avenel, New Jersey. It was at Little Fiddler that the music originated, leading to the creation of this book. Thank you to Kathy Nadjavestky who spent many dedicated hours working on the CD with us. We are grateful to Dianne Raunick and Karen Pinoci for their refinements to the music. Mucho gracias to Ilona Buzick, Bev Claypool, Sue Giachero, and Michael and Sally Struk for their enthusiasm about the original music. A big thank you to Lindy's nieces and nephews who spent their holiday testing out **WWRT: What Went Right Today?**[SM]. We are greatly indebted to Kathy Win who opened her home as a place to write and produce the music. The final recording was done by Mike Nuzzo. Thanks, Mike.

In many ways this book is a miracle. First, Joan wrote the music; then Lindy suggested turning it into a children's book; and when we wondered where we could find a talented illustrator—lo and behold—there was Jim. He just happened to be the father of one of the children enrolled in Little Fiddler Academy. Many thanks to Jim's wife Rose and their two children Marjorie and Quinn for digging out old shoes from the closet and getting Jim started on the illustrations.

To our families and friends, who gave us moral support throughout the project, we are forever grateful.

INTRODUCTION

Children thrive in a supportive environment with lots of positive and loving communication. **WWRT: What Went Right Today?**ᴴ, the book and song combination, was created to generate fun conversations between an adult and a child, about good things that are important in a child's world. This book sparks discussions about topics such as what makes a good day, where your child likes to play, and who your child's friends are. With you as a role model in these discussions, your child will develop skills for seeing the good things and thinking positively.

How to use this book . . .

You will find yourself looking at this wonderfully illustrated book and listening to the **WWRT** song over and over again. The first time you and your child read the book together, enjoy listening to the song as you read through the entire book. The next time around, take your time. Go through one section at a time. **WWRT: What Went Right Today?**ᴴ is grouped into three sections to make it easier to stop for discussion. Discover how simple questions can evolve into a meaningful dialogue. If you and your child are deep in discussion about one subject, feel free to stop and talk. Mission accomplished.

Look at the pictures and take turns answering the questions. First, the adult may answer, which often leads to the child's eagerness to tell a story. The responses to the illustrations and the questions may be endless. We've proposed open-ended questions such as, "What do you like to do in your shoes?" These questions will help you steer the child away from "yes" and "no" answers.

Enjoy the music. The CD includes two versions of the **WWRT** song. The first version includes the questions. The second version is for singing along with while traveling in the car or doing chores around the house. The tune is very catchy. We have found our friends, young and old, singing the **WWRT** song. It reminds us all that so much of life is good.

**We wish you and your child many fond moments
discovering together what went right today.**

Joan Buzick and Lindy Judd

Woke this morning right on time.
I feel great, I feel fine.
Thought of words to make this rhyme.
It's a WWRT Day.

I've got myself a pair of shoes.
They may be old or may be new.
They'll help me do the koo-chi-coo.
It's a WWRT Day.

What went right today?

Who are people I can help?
I help my family, help myself.
Need some help? Just give a yelp!
It's a WWRT Day.

What went right today?

What will make this a good day?

What do you like to do in your shoes?

How can you help yourself
or someone else today?

It's a WWRT . . .
What went right for you and me?
It's a WWRT Day.
What went right today?

It's good old fun to play dress-up,
A marching band coat to button up.
Whoops, I've found my mom's make-up.
It's a WWRT Day.

What went right today?

Look, come look, a place to play!

I've got myself a hideaway.

Here with toys I like to play.

It's a WWRT Day.

What went right today?

Friends can play and we can laugh.
Share a toy then give it back.
We are friends and that's a fact!
It's a WWRT Day.

What went right today?

How do you like to dress-up?

Where are all the places
you like to play?

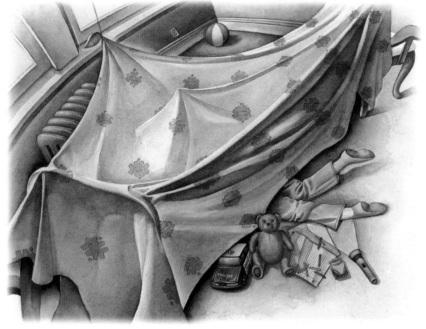

Tell me about your friends.

It's a WWRT . . .
What went right for you and me?
It's a WWRT Day.
What went right today?

What will I be when I grow tall?
Maybe I'll own a shopping mall.
A singer or a dancer in a great big hall?
It's a WWRT Day.
What Went Right Today?

I've a story I can tell.
Listen carefully, listen well.
Once there was a wishing well . . .
It's a WWRT Day.
What Went Right Today?

Friends can play and we can laugh.
Share a toy then give it back.
We are friends and that's a fact!
It's a WWRT Day.

What went right today?

How do you like to dress-up?

Where are all the places
you like to play?

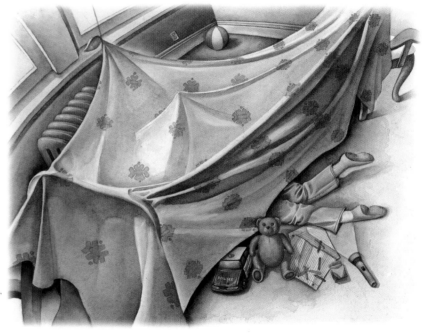

Tell me about your friends.

It's a WWRT . . .
What went right for you and me?
It's a WWRT Day.
What went right today?

What will I be when I grow tall?
Maybe I'll own a shopping mall.
A singer or a dancer in a great big hall?
It's a WWRT Day.
What Went Right Today?

I've a story I can tell.
Listen carefully, listen well.
Once there was a wishing well . . .
It's a WWRT Day.
What Went Right Today?